The Monster of White Bear Lake

Mike Holliday

FishingKids
White Bear Lake, Minnesota

The **Monster** of **White Bear Lake**

FishingKids
PO Box 10590,
White Bear Lake, MN 55110
www.fishingkids.com

Library of Congress Control Number: 2011942300

Credits
Cover and Interior Illustrations
Olga and Aleksey Ivanov

Spinner's Notebook Sketches and Map
Marilyn Emma Anderson

Creative Direction
Megan Derbes McCarthy

Layout and Design
Flat Sole Studio

Printed in the United States of America in Stevens Point, Wisconsin
1220011

Table of Contents

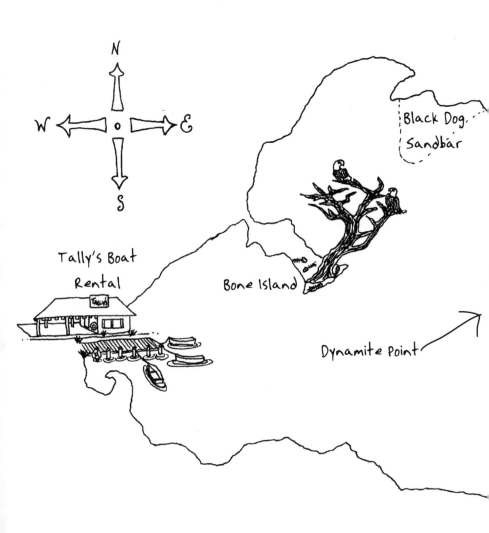

N

W ← o → E

S

Black Dog
Sandbar

Tally's Boat
Rental

TALLY'S

Bone Island

Dynamite Point

White Bear Lake,
Minnesota

Bobber's House

The Creepy
Old Cemetery

Pork Chop Hill

My House

The Chief's House

Of all the seasons of the year, summer is my favorite on White Bear Lake. The lakes in Minnesota freeze over in winter and don't thaw out until late spring. Even though ice fishing is fun, I really like it when I can fish all morning and then jump into the lake to cool off in the afternoon.

The water is different in summer. The surface is warm, but the deeper you go, the colder it gets. If you dive down more than a few feet deep, it'll take your breath away. That's something I do when it's really hot out and the fishing is cold.

I also see a lot more wildlife in summer. In the morning and evening, I can sit on the dock behind our house and watch a pair of eagles fly by. There's also a duck that just had eight ducklings. They live right along shore near the dock. Every morning I walk down there to catch smallmouth bass and watch the ducks swim by.

I'd better introduce myself. My name's Steven Pinner, but everyone in my family and my best friend Bobber call me Spinner. Spinners are my favorite lure in my tackle box and practically my name: S(teven) Pinner.

I should also add, if you haven't already figured it out, my favorite thing in the world is fishing. And to learn as much as I can about fish and how to catch them.

The Chief — that's my grandpa — gave me a special notebook for Christmas so I could write down all the cool fishing stuff that he and my dad tell me. That way I won't forget anything.

There really isn't much for a 10-year old to do in White Bear Lake, Minnesota, besides go fishing, ride bikes or scooters, and skip rocks, which I do down by Dynamite Point. There are a lot of flat rocks there after The Fourth of July Incident.

A few years ago, the town decided to hold the Fourth of July fireworks out on the rocky point on the east side of the lake. That way, people who lived near could watch the show from their houses while other folks could come by boat. Fireman White, who has allergies and is always sneezing, was supposed to shoot off the fireworks.

The Chief said Mr. White is accident prone, and if luck was dynamite, he'd probably blow his nose off. Turns out, The Chief was just about right. When Mr. White went to light the first rocket, he had a sneezing fit and dropped the match into the entire box of rockets and mortars. It was the prettiest and loudest one-minute display of fireworks ever.

Mr. White dove into the water, and it was a good thing he did. When all those fireworks went up with a *BANG!*, rocks and sparks flew everywhere. Now we call the place Dynamite Point, and it has the best skipping rocks on the whole lake.

Chapter 1

The Monster Strikes

Besides great skipping rocks, Dynamite Point has a nice shallow, sandy area in the water. Smallmouths like to swim up from the deeper water to eat minnows there. To get to the Point, I ride my bike over Pork Chop Hill, around the creepy old cemetery, and past my friend Bobber's house.

Bobber is my best friend and fishing buddy. He's not really a good angler, but he is pretty lucky. One time he was casting a crankbait, which is a small lure with two sets of hooks and a plastic lip that makes it dive deep. He stopped reeling to take a drink of soda, and two fish struck his lure at the same time. He reeled them both in, one on each hook.

Bobber calls it The Soda Pop Retrieve. Now, he stops reeling to take a drink of soda whenever he uses a crankbait. Sometimes it works,

13

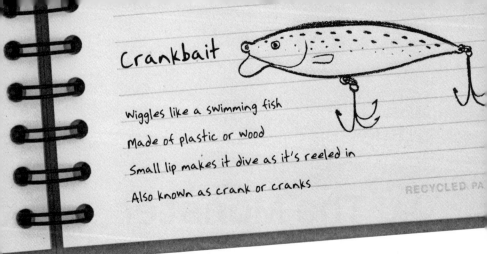

Crankbait

Wiggles like a swimming fish
Made of plastic or wood
Small lip makes it dive as it's reeled in
Also known as crank or cranks

but most of the time, the lure just floats back to the surface, and then he has to start reeling all over again.

Bobber's real name is Bobby Ernest. The Chief gave him the nickname "Bobber" because he's kinda round, and he has this red and white shirt that he likes to wear a lot. It's the same colors as the bobbers we use.

Since I was going by Bobber's house on the way to Dynamite Point, I decided to stop to ask if he wanted to come along. He loves to fish as much as I do, which is every chance I get. When I rode up to his house, he was already down by the lake catching sunfish.

Bobber and I have been friends for a long time, and we like to joke around with each other. I chuckled as I remembered the prank he pulled on me the last time I stopped by.

When I saw Bobber that day, I asked him, "Hey, Bobber, want to go catch some smallies?"

"I'd rather finish making my super secret, totally awesome, all-natural, fish-scented FishingKids Hair Gel," Bobber replied. "I'm going to sell it, get rich, and buy one of those big bass boats. Then I can fish anywhere on the lake."

"Hair gel?" I said. "For fishermen?"

"It's my secret formula. You put it in your hair, and the gel makes your hair hold its shape or stand up in place. It's going to be in every hair salon and house in Washington County," he said.

"Secret formula? What's in it?" I asked.

"I scraped the outer slime coat off the sunfish I caught this morning and mixed it with soda pop and some egg whites. It smells pretty gross, but it's real sticky and dries hard as clay," Bobber explained as he held up his gooey concoction. "Now I just need someone to try it on . . . um . . . Spinner?"

"I'm not putting fish slime in my hair! It stinks like rotten fish," I said while I leaned over and sniffed the hair gel. It smelled like the inside of my grandmother's garbage can.

"Well, someone has to try it, Spinner," Bobber said as he stirred the hair gel with a Popsicle stick. "I came up with the recipe, so I shouldn't have to do everything."

I thought about it for a minute. I mean, how bad could it be? I can wash it out at any time if the smell gets too bad. Maybe it gets better after it dries? And besides, I was already getting used to the odor. It wasn't much worse than my fish-cleaning towel.

"I'll do it if I can have a part of the business," I said. "I want a bass boat, too."

"I dunno, Spinner, it smells awfully gross, and you have a lot more hair than me. It'll probably take the

15

whole bottle," Bobber said. "You'll be fish-smelled, super-held, and hair gelled!" he added with a laugh.

"I don't care if it takes two bottles," I said, and I emptied the entire bottle onto my head. It felt kind of like warm Jell-O, only stickier and stinkier.

"It'll be pretty gooey until it dries," Bobber said. "Maybe we should shape it, before it hardens. How about combing your hair into a big dorsal fin, like on the back of a fish?"

"That would be cool. Then we'll know if it holds up to the wind as I ride my bike home," I said.

I put each hand on the side of my head, and using my fingers as a comb, I pulled my hair upwards until my palms met. After several tries, all my hair was pointing up like the dorsal fin of a fish. I checked my reflection in the lake. I must admit, it looked pretty cool. Maybe ol' Bobber was on to something.

"Perfect," Bobber said. "You're the fishiest Hair Gel Fin Boy on White Bear Lake!"

I hopped on my bike and started pedaling up Pork Chop Hill, which is a big, winding hill between my house and Bobber's. He named it that because it looked like a pork chop Bobber had for dinner one night. If you ask me, I think he just didn't have enough to eat that day and had pork chops on the brain, but that's what we still call it to this day.

It was a long, slow ride up the hill with the wind blowing in my face. I couldn't smell the hair gel any more, probably because the wind was blowing so hard. I was about halfway up the hill when I looked back to see how far I'd gone. That's when I saw the cats chasing me.

That's funny, I thought as I looked at all those cats running behind me. I wondered why . . .
Oh no, fish hair!

It seemed like every cat in the neighborhood was trying to catch me. Even Mrs. Brown's big, hairy orange tabby. I didn't even know that cat could even run!

I started peddling hard, hoping to get away. I rode my bike like my life depended on it. The cats were about to pounce as I reached the top of the hill. The wind wasn't in my face any more, and I was on flat ground, so I quickly sped away from them.

"Whew, that was close," I said under my breath. I could have been licked bald by an army of cats!

When I got home, my hair was still standing up in a point like a fish fin, and like the other cats, my pet cat Scooter kept following me around the house. Mom was in the kitchen making dinner, so I walked in to show off my new look. I just knew everyone in town would want to have FishingKids Hair Gel.

"Hi, Mom. I'm back from fishing," I said as I walked into the kitchen.

"Spinner, can you set the table and . . . what's that smell?" she asked. "And what happened to your hair?"

"It's our new FishingKids Hair Gel. Bobber and I are going to get rich and buy bass boats and go fishing every day from now until forever," I said.

Just then, Scooter jumped onto the counter behind me and started licking my head. And at that moment, it hit me — Bobber had pulled a fast one on me.

I had to wash my hair ten times, and it still took three days for my hair to look normal again. Mom didn't think Bobber's joke was so funny, but he and I shared a snack and laughed about it all afternoon. Fish slime for hair gel — that is pretty funny.

So today when I stopped by, Bobber was already down on the dock fishing. I parked my bike under the old elm tree on the side of his house.

"Hey, Bobber, catch anything?" I shouted.

"Lots of sunfish. Look, I've got one! I've got one!" he squealed as his bobber disappeared under the water. "I've got my magic-casting-sunfish catcher working now. I'm the Sunfish King of the World!"

"What are you using to catch them?" I asked.

"Worms and a red and white bobber. That's my best rig for catching sunfish," he said, "but don't tell

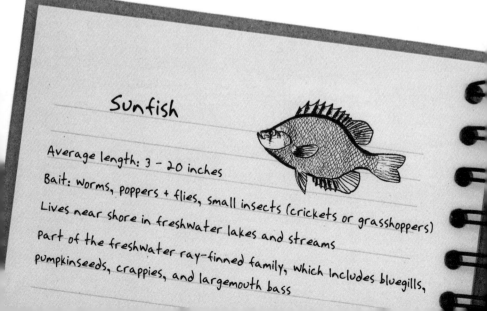

Sunfish

Average length: 3 - 20 inches

Bait: Worms, poppers + flies, small insects (crickets or grasshoppers)

Lives near shore in freshwater lakes and streams

Part of the freshwater ray-finned family, which includes bluegills, pumpkinseeds, crappies, and largemouth bass anyone, or they'll want to be the Sunfish King, too, and use my rig."

I just smiled. Everyone uses worms and a bobber to catch sunfish. It's the best way to catch them.

As Bobber was reeling in the sunfish, there was a huge explosion of water. Bobber's rod bent double. He yanked too hard and knocked his hat off his head with his fishing rod, and then the line snapped.

"What was that?" I asked.

"It was a super crazy fish missile with giant teeth and a rocket tail! It was dark and scary, and it ate my sunfish in one gulp!" yelled Bobber.

"Slow down Bobber, you're talking too fast," I said. Bobber always talks too fast when he gets excited.

"It was some kind of monster! It ate my sunfish," said Bobber. "It was dark and long and . . . and . . . HUGE!"

Chapter 2

Ask the Chief

The next morning, I went down to the dock to fish while I waited for The Chief to wake up. He would know about any monsters in the lake. He knows practically everything about White Bear Lake.

I was casting a rubber worm for smallmouth bass when the mother duck and her babies paddled up to the dock. Something was missing. Instead of eight baby ducklings, there were only seven. The mother duck looked sad.

A couple casts later, a smallmouth ate my worm and made a mad dash for the dock pilings. I was able to stop it before it could wrap my line around the metal poles, then I reeled it to the surface. I was removing the hook when I

Smallmouth Bass

Average length: 10 – 16 inches   Average Weight: 1 – 4 pounds

Bait: curly-tailed jigs, crankbaits, spinner baits, plastic worms

Lives in fresh water lakes and rivers

Has a short jaw that doesn't go past its eyes

Also known as smallies, bronze backs, or brown bass

heard a door slam shut, and The Chief stepped out onto the back deck of the house.

The Chief is my dad's dad, and he grew up on White Bear Lake. He was an engineer and helped design a lot of the bridges in Minnesota. So he has a lot of friends and has been around the water most of his life. He's also the best fisherman I know, which is great because he lives next door.

The Chief told me that he once won a walleye tournament using nothing but a hammer and a can of peas. He cut a big hole in the ice and would drop a pea into the water. When a walleye came up to eat it, The Chief would bang it on the head with his hammer. He caught over 100 pounds of walleye that day.

Mom says the story isn't true. That walleyes don't eat peas. But The Chief has a big ol' stuffed walleye on the wall of his house, and that walleye has a flat spot on its head. Underneath the walleye is a plate that says "White Bear Lake Walleye Champ of 1978."

Walleye

Average length: 12 - 18 inches   Average Weight: 1 - 4 pounds
Bait: jigs with minnows, leeches
Most popular game fish in the U.S.
Has big marble-like eyes that reflect light and help them see
at night when they feed

RECYCLED PAPER

When I heard The Chief come outside, I put my fishing gear away. Then I ran up the steps to the house. I wanted to ask him about monsters in White Bear Lake.

"Hey, Chief, what'cha doing?" I asked.

"Reading the paper," he said. "It's a little cool this morning, Spinner. Try a lipped plug and cast it towards the weed bed off the end of the dock. Should be some nice smallies eating minnows right about now."

"Um, sir, I have a question I'd like to ask you," I said. "Yesterday, Bobber was reeling in a sunfish, and something ate it. It broke his line. We never got a good look at it, but it was big like a shark or a sturgeon."

"Well, Spinner, the last I looked Minnesota was shark-free, and it wasn't likely a sturgeon up in the shallows around Bobber's dock. It could have been a big bass," he said.

"It was way larger than a bass, Chief. It made a splash as big as a wheelbarrow," I said.

"Hmm, a fish that big can only be one thing, a muskellunge. They're the biggest fish in White Bear Lake," said the Chief.

"A muskie. Wow!"

"Yep, Bobber, probably tied into a big one. Maybe even Old Sam," said The Chief.

"Who's Old Sam?" I asked.

"Old Sam is the biggest muskellunge you've ever seen. He's more than four feet long and mean as a crocodile," said The Chief. "He's got teeth as long as your fingers and can bite your hand off. Oh, he's a mean one alright."

"I hooked him off the dock one time," said The Chief. "I bet he weighed fifty pounds. He bit through my line and then looked like he was laughing as he swam away. That was about three years ago."

"Wow! I never caught a muskie," I said. "That would be beyond cool."

"Get out your notebook, Spinner, and I'll tell you all about White Bear Lake monsters."

Chapter 3

Fishing for Monsters

"**M**uskies swim into the shallows in the summer," said The Chief as he pointed to the dock. "They like to hang out around the weed beds like the one off the end of the dock. They eat the fish swimming in and out of the weeds."

"Do you think that it was Old Sam that Bobber hooked?" I asked.

"Not likely," said The Chief. "It could have been any old muskie. I haven't heard about anyone hooking Old Sam in over a year. Some fella from the city was fishing in one of the rental boats from Tally's and hooked him off Manitou Island. Broke his rod in half, and Old Sam got away again."

In the last year or so, The Chief's legs have gotten kind of wobbly, so he sits down a lot more. When I was just a kid, The Chief and I would go for long walks in the woods around White Bear Lake and talk about

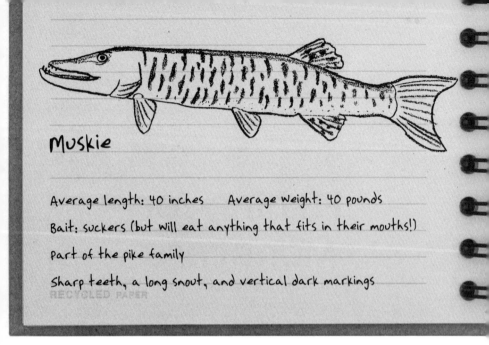

Muskie

Average length: 40 inches   Average weight: 40 pounds
Bait: suckers (but will eat anything that fits in their mouths!)
Part of the pike family
Sharp teeth, a long snout, and vertical dark markings

fishing. Now he does most of his talking from his rocking chair on the porch. The Chief was rocking real fast in his chair now, which is something he does when he gets real excited.

"Where's Manitou Island?" I asked.

"You and Bobber call it Bone Island. But Manitou Island is its real name," said The Chief. "According to legend, Manitou is the great Indian spirit who appeared as a white bear and made this lake."

"That's where the eagle's nest is," I said. "Bobber and I were walking along the shoreline and saw fish bones everywhere. It was scary and cool at the same time."

The Chief stopped rocking. He pulled out the map of White Bear Lake that he always kept on the table and pointed to where the eagle's nest was located.

"Were the fish bones near the eagle's nest?" asked The Chief.

26

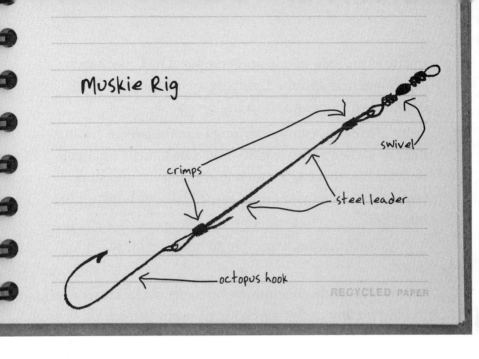

Muskie Rig

crimps

swivel

steel leader

octopus hook

RECYCLED PAPER

"Kind of, about 200 yards away," I replied, showing The Chief the spot on the map. "Right on the shore by the giant elm tree that hangs over the water."

"That's probably where the eagles eat their meals," said The Chief. "The bones probably fall from that tree. The Indians would call it a very sacred place."

"Do they have muskies there?" I asked.

"Probably," said The Chief. "The shoreline is shallow and there's a big sandbar off the end of the island. Muskies like that kind of stuff."

"Now get your fishing notebook, Spinner, and I'll tell you how to rig for one."

Inside my fishing notebook, I've got drawings of rigs for catching bluegills — we call them sunfish, plus

Fishing Notebook by S. Pinner

smallmouth bass, perch, and crappie. The Chief's secret slip-bobber rig and the Lindy rig are all in there. I've even drawn all my knots in my notebook.

"Muskies can bite through monofilament fishing line, so we use a steel leader," said The Chief. "First you tie your line to a swivel, then crimp a 40-pound steel leader to it. Then you crimp a 4/0 Octopus hook on the other end."

"Isn't that hook too big to hook a sunfish?" I asked.

"Good observation, Spinner," said The Chief. "It's too big for any of the sunfish family, but perfect for suckers — the muskie's favorite food."

"Wow, there are a lot of suckers around Bobber's dock. We catch them all the time," I said.

I smiled as I thought about all the muskie bait Bobber and I had caught from the dock over the years. We usually just let the suckers go. This time, we'll use them to catch a monster.

"Then it probably was a muskie that ate his sunfish," said The Chief. "They'll eat practically anything that moves. Even birds."

Chapter 4

Chasing Monsters

After The Chief showed me how to make his secret muskie rig, I asked Dad to take me to Tally's. I wanted to buy some steel leaders, crimps, and hooks. Later, I made my own rigs, tied them on my heaviest rod, and headed over to Bobber's house. When I got there, Bobber was in his backyard turning over big rocks.

"Hey, Bobber, what are you doing?" I asked.

"Diggin' for worms," he said. "You gotta look under the rocks during the daytime. They like to be cool."

Bobber flipped over a rock and grabbed a worm that was trying to escape into its hole. He pulled and pulled, but the worm

was slippery and he lost his grip, falling backwards into the leaves.

"That was a superworm," said Bobber. "It had super-slimy hole-gripping powers."

"Can't you just buy worms at Tally's?" I asked.

Tally's Tackle Shop and Marina is right on the water, and besides serving food and drinks, they rent boats and are the best tackle and live bait shop on White Bear Lake.

"Yeah, but I like to catch my own wigglers and nightcrawlers and such," he said, patting his front pants pocket. "Got a pocketful already. Gonna use them to catch bass and walleye later."

"I usually put them into a cup or can," I said. "That's how they sell them at Tally's, in a cup full of dirt. Not your pocket!"

"Yeah, they keep that cup in the refrigerator. That keeps them cool. You can also put them in a cooler with some ice in it. Just don't let the water get on them, or they'll get all soggy and die," explained Bobber. "But I don't have a cup to put the worms in right now, so I'm keeping them cool in my pocket."

"Okay," I said as I watched Bobber flip over a rock, catch a worm, and stuff it into his pocket. I thought about telling him that if he sits down with worms in his pocket he was going to have worm stew in his shorts. I bet his mom has already seen worm dirt in the laundry.

"The Chief said that fish you hooked yesterday was probably a muskie," I said. "Maybe even Old Sam."

"Naw, I think it was an alligator that got loose from the zoo or was someone's pet and got away," he said. "I once saw a TV show about an alligator that lived in the sewers."

An alligator? In Minnesota? I saw the same show that Bobber did about alligators, but they were in the sewers of New York City. Bobber has some imagination. He's always stretching the truth, which The Chief says makes him a good fisherman.

Bobber was trying to flip over a big rock and having a hard time. So I got a thick tree branch, stuck it under the rock, and helped him flip it over. Using a branch or pole creates leverage. It's called a fulcrum, and it makes moving things a lot easier.

Under the giant rock was the motherload of worms. Bobber used both hands to shove worms into his pocket as fast as he could.

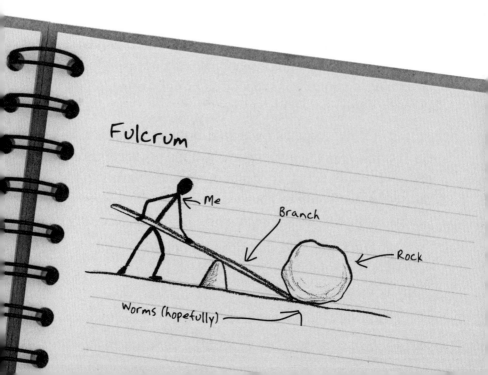

Fulcrum

Me

Branch

Rock

Worms (hopefully)

"That was in New York," I replied. "And it was a long time ago, and probably not even real. No one has ever seen an alligator in White Bear Lake."

"Maybe it only comes out at night. Maybe it has super x-ray night vision and can hold its breath for days, so it doesn't have to come to the surface."

"Bobber, alligators don't have super x-ray night vision, and they can only hold their breath for about an hour. Don't you remember reading about alligators in Mrs. Gunderson's class?"

Mrs. Gunderson was our second grade teacher. She had all kinds of books about countries, and space, and people. Bobber and I liked to read the ones about fish and animals.

"I guess. But someone could have had a pet alligator, and it got away," said Bobber.

"An alligator? In White Bear Lake? Seriously?"

"It could be true. It could live in an underwater cave or beneath someone's dock. It only comes out at night to eat fish and ducks," said Bobber.

"Ducks? Hmm," I said as I thought about the missing duckling from this morning.

Chapter 5

A Sucker Born Every Minute

Bobber really had me worried that there might be an alligator in White Bear Lake. No alligator had ever been seen in Minnesota before, but it could have been someone's pet that escaped.

"We need to find out what that monster is," I told Bobber, "whether it's a fish or an alligator."

"How do we to do that, Spinner?"

"We'll catch some suckers and use them for bait. Everything eats suckers, even my cat Scooter."

"Cool," said Bobber. "We can use the worms I just caught." He pulled out a handful of wiggling worms and dirt from his pocket.

We spent the rest of the morning fishing for suckers. Luckily, I had my fishing notebook with me, and The Chief had told me all about catching suckers.

They're everywhere in White Bear Lake and fight like crazy. I couldn't wait to catch one and use it for bait.

There's a reason they call them suckers. They have big lips and a mouth that points down. They like to "suck" food off the bottom. The Chief calls them the lake's vacuum cleaners.

I took out my fishing notebook and turned to the page about catching suckers. According to The Chief, you want to use a #4 hook with three or four split shots about 15 inches above the hook. That's just enough weight to bring the bait to the bottom of the lake. You run the hook through the worm three or four times, so the fish can't pull it off the hook.

Bobber and I rigged our spinning rods for suckers, baited up with worms, and cast out over the gravel bar between his dock and the floating dock next door. While we waited for a bite, Bobber talked more about keeping worms fresh.

Suckers

Average length: 16 inches   Average weight: 2 – 3 pounds
Bait: Worms, bread (and good to use as bait!)
Suckers have thick, fleshy lips which they use to "suck" up food
They feed on the bottom of lakes and rivers

"Yep, you've got to keep the worms cool if you want them to be lively," he said. "You can't just let them sit in the sun, or they'll fry hard as string beans."

We fished all morning and never got a bite from a sucker, although we did catch two nice largemouth bass that Bobber kept for dinner.

We brought the fish up to Bobber's house for his father to clean. Bobber's dad designs electronics and works out of the house. He's a really good fisherman, but kind of scatterbrained and always forgetting things. He works all the time, so he can't go fishing much, but he sure does like to eat fish. Bobber's mom and dad will really be happy that he brought home dinner.

While we were putting the bass in a cooler and adding ice, we made other plans to catch some suckers to use for bait.

"I'll come over to your house tomorrow," said Bobber. "Maybe your dock is better for sucker fishing."

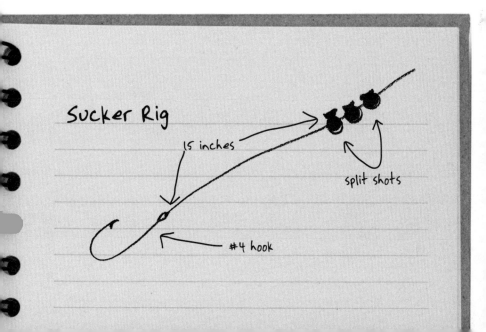

Sucker Rig
15 inches
split shots
#4 hook

"Great idea, Bobber," I said. "I can ask The Chief. He'll know where to catch them."

"I put the worms in a plastic butter container I got out of the recycling bin. Put them in your refrigerator, and we'll have fresh, lively worms for bait in the morning," he said as he handed me the butter container.

"If we catch a sucker at my dock, Bobber, we have to use him for bait right there," I said. "We can't carry a sucker over to your house by bike."

"Okay," said Bobber. "Tomorrow, we catch suckers, then use them to catch a monster."

Chapter 6

Fishin' for Suckers

That night, I looked up suckers on the Internet. The article I found said they like water that's between 55 and 65 degrees Fahrenheit.

When I got up the next morning, I went down to the dock with my thermometer to test the water temperature. The Chief came down and asked what I was doing.

"I'm checking the water temperature, sir," I said as I pulled the thermometer out of the water and looked at it. "I read that suckers like a certain temperature."

"Well, you'll want to check the temperature on the bottom, not the surface," The Chief said. "Suckers live and eat on the bottom of the lake where it's a lot colder than on the surface."

"Oh, yeah!" I said.

The Chief helped me tie my thermometer to a string and attached a weight so it would sink to the bottom of the lake. We let it sit there a few minutes and then pulled it up.

"61 degrees. That's perfect!" I said.

Just then, we heard a loud crash and a scream, and Mom came running out of the house.

"Worms! There are worms in my butter!" she yelled. "I hate worms!"

The Chief just kind of smiled and looked at me. I lowered my head.

"Steven Pinner, you get in the kitchen right this minute and clean all those worms off my nice clean floor," she said. "And I don't ever want to see worms in my refrigerator again."

"Yes ma'am," I replied as I headed up the steps. "Bobber and I just wanted to use them to catch suckers."

My mom shook her head. "Well, Bobber sure suckered you into scaring your mother," she said. "You'd be in a world of trouble if I had put those worms on my toast."

As I headed up the steps, I saw the mother duck and her ducklings swimming by the dock. I counted them: one, two, three, four, five, six . . . six! Two days ago there were eight ducklings. Then seven. Now six! Something was definitely eating the baby ducks.

I thought about the ducklings and the poor mother duck as I ran into the house to pick worms up off the kitchen floor. I knew an eagle would sometimes eat ducklings. But so could an alligator!

If the eagles that flew by the dock every morning weren't eating the ducks, then it must be the monster. And it was eating everything between Bobber's house and mine. I needed to solve the mystery of The Monster of White Bear Lake, and I needed to do it quick.

And I had just the plan.

Chapter 7

The Monster Trap

When Bobber arrived, I was down in the basement looking through The Chief's duck decoys. Decoys are fake ducks made out of plastic that float and have a weight and string on them to keep them in place. I found the smallest decoy of the bunch and tied it to my fishing rod.

"Hey, Spinner," said Bobber. "What are you doing with those?"

"I'm going to set a trap for The Monster of White Bear Lake. When it tries to eat this decoy, I'm going to take a photo of it," I said, holding up my dad's camera. "We can make a fort out of cardboard boxes, put it on the dock, and hide in it while we wait for the monster to attack the duck decoy. Then, I'll jump up and snap a picture of it."

"Wow, crazy cool plan! I want to help," said Bobber.

"You can wade out and pull the decoy through the dock pilings. Then come back and hide with me," I offered. "You can also hold the camera while I reel in the decoy. I'll bet our picture will be in all the papers."

Bobber hesitated. "Um, Spinner? What if the monster attacks when I'm walking around the docks with the decoy?"

"Don't be silly, Bobber. Alligators and such are called man eaters. You're just a boy. They don't call them boy eaters."

"Oh, that's good," said Bobber, smiling a little.

Once we had the decoy ready, we headed back upstairs. We went to the garage to look for cardboard to make a fort. We found two large boxes and some duct tape.

When I turned nine, The Chief gave me a pocket knife and said, "Remember this, Spinner. A man with a knife is worth a dollar an hour more." I think that means you can do a lot of things with a pocket knife, like open boxes, cut string, and clean fish. I was sure glad I had my knife, even though it only has one blade.

"If I cut the side off one box, we can use it for a roof on the other box," I explained to Bobber, and I used the pocket knife to cut the box. "Then we'll cut small peep holes in the side, so we can see out."

"Whoa, crazy cool fort," said Bobber. "You're really good at making things, Spinner."

"That's because my dad's an engineer."

"Your dad drives a train?" asked Bobber. "I thought he helped build bridges like The Chief did."

I stopped cutting and looked at Bobber. He's a good friend, but sometimes he can be kind of goofy with his thinking.

"Geez, Bobber, he does design bridges. An engineer is someone who designs and builds things. Although an engineer can also be the name for the person who drives a train. Now come on, let's put the fort on the dock."

Bobber and I took the cardboard fort and the spinning rod with plastic duck decoy down to the dock. Then I climbed into the fort while Bobber waded into the water and wove the decoy through the dock pilings and along the shoreline. When he got three docks away, all the line was off the reel.

"Hey Bobber," I shouted. "Come on back to the fort. It's time to hide and wait for the monster!"

Chapter 8

Spinner Gets a Bite

Bobber and I sat in the box fort for half an hour, watching the decoy through the peep holes. Nothing happened, and we were getting restless when Bobber spied the eagle flying towards the dock.

"Look, Spinner, the bald eagle is coming our way," he said, pointing towards Pork Chop Hill. "I'll bet it grabs the decoy with its feet."

"Talons, Bobber. Eagles have talons, like long nails on their feet, that they use to grab fish and other prey," I said, opening and closing my hand nervously. We were going to learn whether eagles were eating the ducklings.

Bobber and I watched through the peep hole as I turned the handle on the spinning reel. The duck decoy slowly moved out from under our neighbor's dock. I reeled the decoy into the open, and then stopped it there

for the eagle to see. This was going to be the easiest meal that eagle ever caught.

The eagle was almost to the dock when it saw the decoy. We could see it look under its wing at what it must have thought was a small duck. It turned towards the dock and then . . . flew away.

"Aw, booger pops," said Bobber. "It flew right on by. It didn't even try to eat the decoy."

Bobber was right. The eagle saw the decoy, but it didn't show any interest in eating a duckling.

"Well, that eliminates one possible monster," I said as I began to reel the decoy back towards our dock fort. Maybe later, Bobber and I would be able to try again. Right now, I wanted to go to see if we could catch any suckers off my dock.

First, I had to reel the decoy in and then put it away. I had reeled the decoy almost to the dock, and Bobber was using my dad's camera to take a picture of the decoy next to the dock, when everything exploded. A giant fish leaped from the water and tried to eat the decoy.

"It's the monster!" yelled Bobber. He turned to run and then fell against the wall of the cardboard fort.

When Bobber fell, it knocked me backwards, and Bobber, the fort, my fishing rod, and I all rolled off the dock. We hit the water with a loud *SPLASH!*

"Don't let the monster eat me, Spinner!" yelled Bobber, and he struggled to untangle his legs and stand up. By that time, I had gotten to my feet and realized that when we fell the line broke. The decoy was just floating next to us.

"Bobber, you can stand up. It's only two feet deep," I shouted as I watched Bobber try to swim-run to shore. "It's a muskie, Bobber. The monster is a muskie! I got a good look at it."

"I might have gotten a picture of it," added Bobber, and for the first time, I remembered my dad's camera.

I looked around. The only thing still on the dock was the tackle box I had been sitting on. Then I looked down, and there in the water was Dad's camera.

Chapter 9

Muskie Trouble

I reached into the water and lifted my dad's camera off the bottom. Then I pointed the camera at Bobber and pushed the button to take a picture. Water came out of the lens.

"Oh no, my dad's camera. It's ruined," I said as Bobber and I stood on the shore next to the dock. "I'm going to be in so much trouble. He doesn't even know I borrowed it."

"If your dad grounds you for life, Spinner, can I have your fishing rods?" asked Bobber, pointing to the rod in my hand. "You won't need them any more."

"Cut it out, Bobber. It's not funny. I have to go tell him. He's going to be really disappointed."

Bobber and I walked back up to the house carrying the fishing rod, decoy, tackle box, and dripping wet camera. When we got there, Dad was just pulling into the driveway. He got out of his car to greet us.

"Hi, Bobber. Hey, Spinner. How'd you boys get so wet?" he asked as he pulled his briefcase out of the car.

"It's the monster!" shouted Bobber, waving his hands in big excited circles. "He ate the decoy and drowned your camera. I think I got a photo of it. Honestly, Mr. Pinner, the monster did it."

"The what?" asked Dad. "Bobber, slow down. Tell me exactly what happened."

We took our time and told Dad about the fort, the decoy, and our plan to discover what was eating the ducklings near the dock. When we got to the part about falling into the water and all our stuff, including Dad's camera, going in with us, he just shook his head and laughed.

"You boys are lucky you didn't get hurt," he said. "I'm glad you're alright. Now about that camera . . ."

Dad took the news better than I thought. His digital camera was kind of old, but he said he would try to fix it. That's what engineers do — they build and fix things. If it couldn't be fixed, he would pay me five dollars every time I washed his car or The Chief's truck until I could buy a new one. I figured it would take about 25 buckets of soap to pay for a new camera.

We went into the kitchen, and Dad opened a couple of bottles of juice and gave them to Bobber and me. Right then, The Chief walked in, and we told him all about the decoy-eating muskie, and the photo we

took that would have proved it if the camera hadn't gotten ruined.

"You boys sure have done your homework," said The Chief as he picked up Dad's camera and examined it. "Let's put the boat in tomorrow and see if we can catch some suckers for bait. It's time you boys caught yourselves a monster."

"Really, Chief?" I said, trying to hide my excitement. "You'll take us muskie fishing?"

"You and Bobber put a lot of time and effort into figuring out what's eating those ducklings. I'll bet it's the same muskie that Bobber hooked off his dock. They're territorial, so they live and feed in the same places all the time. That makes it easy for us to know where they'll be," explained The Chief as he walked outside with Dad's camera in hand.

Bobber and I followed The Chief outside.

"I'm proud of your honesty, Spinner," said The Chief, looking at the camera in his hand. "You knew you did something wrong, but you immediately told your dad about it instead of trying to hide the truth. Honesty like that deserves a reward, and catching that muskie will be the best thing I can give to you two."

Chapter 10

Spinner Hooks a Monster

The Chief's boat isn't one of those fancy fiberglass bass boats with glitter paint and a giant engine. It's really just set up for fishing. It's an aluminum hull bass boat with carpet and rod holders and a livewell, which is a space where a pump pulls in fresh water to give oxygen to the fish kept there. That's where we'll put the suckers to keep them alive.

Live Well

Tank for keeping bait and fish alive
Fresh water is pumped into the live
well to provide oxygen for the fish.

His boat is the best. It has a trolling motor and depth finder and everything. We were sure to catch a muskie now.

Bobber and I were waiting at the dock when The Chief came down.

"Okay, boys. I usually just use a net called a minnow seine to catch small bait fish near shore," said The Chief as he lowered his boat into the water. "But since you're fishing for Old Sam, we'll need to catch some larger suckers. I'm going to take you to one of my secret fishing holes. It's right off Black Dog Sandbar, and you can't ever tell anyone about it."

"We won't, Chief. I promise," I said, nudging Bobber with an elbow.

"I promise, too. I won't tell anyone, even if I'm captured by ninja-zombie pirates, and they threaten to boil me in oil and eat my brain," said Bobber.

The Chief just smiled.

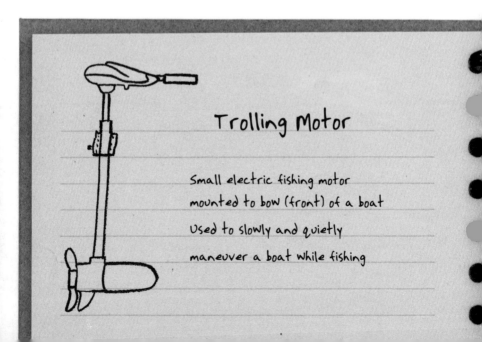

Trolling Motor

Small electric fishing motor mounted to bow (front) of a boat
Used to slowly and quietly maneuver a boat while fishing

"If ninja-zombie pirates grab you, Bobber, it's okay to talk," he said. "Tell them that the FishingKids crankbait stuck in your shoe is our secret Shoe Bait. That will throw them off."

Bobber and I looked down at his shoes. He liked to wear those soft plastic Crocs with holes in them. He's always accidently ending up in the lake, and the water drains right out of the them. Hooked to the top of his left shoe was a lure.

"Hey, I wonder when that got stuck there," said Bobber. "It's my lucky crankbait. I thought I lost it."

"Well, now it's your Lucky Shoe Bait," I said. "You'll always have it with you when you need a lure."

"Yeah, I kind of like it there," said Bobber, smiling. "It looks totally crazy fish head cool."

"You boys need to get your totally crazy fish head cool carcasses in the boat if you want to catch a muskie

Depth Finder

Sonar device that tells how deep the water is

Some depth finders can locate fish

Also called depth recorder and fishfinder

before dark," said
The Chief as he
helped Bobber and
me aboard. "Put your
life jackets on, and pick a
seat. We're heading for Black
Dog Sandbar."

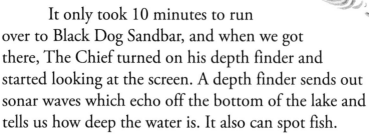

It only took 10 minutes to run
over to Black Dog Sandbar, and when we got
there, The Chief turned on his depth finder and
started looking at the screen. A depth finder sends out
sonar waves which echo off the bottom of the lake and
tells us how deep the water is. It also can spot fish.

When The Chief found the 40-foot hole that was
his secret fishing hole, he took the engine out of gear,
turned it off, and picked up the anchor.

"We'll anchor up here," said The Chief as he
tossed the anchor overboard and then tied off the line.
"I see a school of suckers near the bottom on the depth
recorder. Grab a rod, boys. We're going to catch our
bait!"

In 20 minutes, we had five suckers in the livewell.
I caught two, and Bobber three. He says he caught more
because he was rubbing his new Shoe Bait for luck.

"We've got bait. Now let's see if we can catch a
muskie, boys," said The Chief as he gunned the throttle
and pointed the boat back to his dock.

When we got near the dock, The Chief dropped
anchor. He then rigged up two rods with his special
muskie rig. He hooked two suckers through the nose
and cast them out near the weed bed where the ducks

live. Bobber and I were telling The Chief about decoy fishing when Bobber's line pulled tight.

"I've got the sucker-eating muskie monster," shouted Bobber as he pulled back on his rod. He set the hook so hard he knocked the cap off his head. "I'm the Sucker Bait Monster Muskie King of White Bear Lake!"

Bobber lifted his rod and reeled down, taking up line and playing the fish like a pro, but something was wrong. The fish was coming in too easily.

When it swam close to the boat, The Chief stood up and got a good look at it. Bobber lifted the fish's head out of the water while it splashed its tail beside the boat.

"It's a northern pike, Bobber, not a muskie," said The Chief. He leaned over and grabbed Bobber's line. "It's only about 26 inches long and looks a lot like a muskie, but it's no monster. It's good to eat, though, so we'll keep it for dinner."

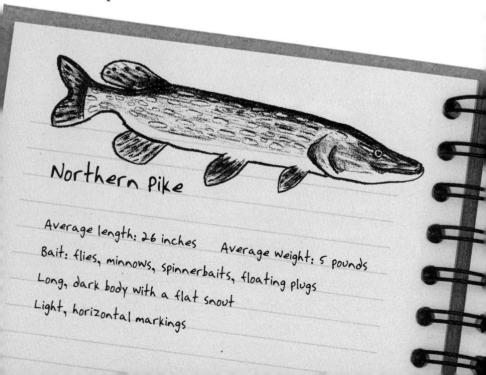

Northern Pike

Average length: 26 inches   Average weight: 5 pounds
Bait: flies, minnows, spinnerbaits, floating plugs
Long, dark body with a flat snout
Light, horizontal markings

The Chief lifted the northern into the boat and then used his pliers to get the hook out of the pike's tooth-filled mouth. He put the fish in the cooler, and told Bobber what a great job he did reeling in the fish, even though he did set the hook a bit too hard.

The Chief put another live sucker on for Bobber and then cast it out. A little while went by, and Bobber remembered he still had some worms in his pocket. He was taking the squished worms out and tossing them overboard when my line started to pull tight.

"I've got a big one, Chief!" I screamed. The rod bent over and line screamed off the reel. "I've got a monster!"

Chapter 11

Monster Wrestling

"It's a Monster, Chief!" I yelled. I held on to the rod with all my might. "Help me, Chief. He's going to take the rod away from me."

The Chief slid over and put his hand on the fishing rod. He pulled back, easing the pressure on my wrists. Line was coming off the reel and making the drag scream.

R-r-r-r-r-r-r-r-r-r-r went the reel as the big fish pulled out more line.

"It's a giant! It's a monster! It's a crazy fish! It's a giant monster crazy fish!" hooted Bobber as he pointed at the fish swimming across the surface.

After a long run, the fish stopped. I could feel it shaking its head back and forth.

"He's trying to shake the hook free, Spinner," said The Chief. "Pull back and reel down, and we'll get some of that line back. From the length of that first run, he's a big one."

With the help of The Chief, I played the fish, gaining line as I reeled it closer to the boat. The muskie was so strong it almost took the rod out of my hands when it swam away. The Chief helped me by holding the rod and coaching me on when to reel and when to let the fish take line.

On one run, the fish almost swam around a dock piling, which could cut the line and let the muskie escape. The Chief pulled back on the rod and told me, "Reel fast," and we stopped it before it got to the dock.

The fish made two more runs, each shorter than the next. When it came to the surface near the boat, Bobber stood up and pointed.

"That's the biggest monster fish in the world!" he said.

"It's a muskie, all right" said The Chief. "Keep calm, Spinner. You've got it."

I pulled back on the rod to gain line and then reeled some more. After 15 minutes, the fish was right next to the boat. The Chief then opened a hatch and pulled out the biggest landing net I've ever seen.

"That's a big net, Chief," said Bobber. "You could catch every monster muskie in the lake with that."

"Okay, Spinner," said The Chief. "I want you to gently guide the fish closer to the boat. Then I'll net it."

The muskie looked tired. I pulled as hard as I could, and the giant fish swam right alongside the boat. It looked nearly as long as I was tall.

I lifted the rod again, and as the fish moved forward . . . *WHOOSH!* The Chief scooped it into the net. He hoisted the fish out of the water, and Bobber started to dance.

"It's the giant monster crazy muskie fish of White Bear Lake!" yelled Bobber as he bounced from one foot to the other. "Look at those teeth!"

The muskie looked mean — all five feet of him. He was green and pointed like an arrow, with a mossy-green back and a mouth full of razor sharp teeth that he kept opening and closing.

He tried to bite the net. Then he wiggled back and forth. The Chief held the net over the water, waiting for the fish to calm down. Then he pulled it into the boat, setting the fish and the net on the deck.

"It's Old Sam alright," said The Chief as he worked the hook free. "I can tell by the scar on his nose. He got that from an eagle when he was small. It's been with him ever since."

"Wow, Spinner, you caught Old Sam. You're going to be a hero," said Bobber. "We're going to be monster fishing magazine superstars!"

"I don't know about that, Bobber," said The Chief. "But you will probably get your picture in the paper if you decide to keep him. We'll have to kill Old Sam if we're going to take him to Tally's for a photo."

"Kill him?" I said, with a gulp. "I never thought about killing him. I just wanted to find out what was happening to the ducklings."

Chapter 12

Life or Death

The Chief picked up the big muskie by its gills to make sure the fish couldn't bite him. He slid one hand under the fish's belly and held it sideways.

"I'd say he's close to 50 pounds, Spinner," said The Chief. "He's a big one. Bigger than any muskie I've ever caught."

I leaned over and looked closer at the giant muskie. When he was out of the water and in The Chief's hands, Old Sam didn't look so mean.

I touched him and felt the fish shake. It made me think about how long this fish had lived in White Bear Lake. He's been around longer than me.

"How old do you think he is, Chief?" I asked while Bobber poked the fish's belly.

"He's an old one," said The Chief as he looked closely at the fish. "He could be over 20 years."

The fish looked less like a monster now, although he did have some mean-looking teeth. When I thought about killing Old Sam, I felt kind of bad, even if he was eating the baby ducks.

"Do we have to kill it, Chief?" I asked, thinking that when the fish closed its mouth, it kind of made a frown. "He looks sad."

"It's up to you, Spinner," said The Chief. "We have to kill Old Sam if we're going to take him to Tally's for a photo. There's nothing wrong with killing a fish as long as you're planning to eat it."

"If you kill Old Sam, then you'll be known as The Monster Hunter of White Bear Lake," said Bobber with awe. "You'll be famous. Everyone will know your name."

"It's sure to make the paper," said The Chief. "The *White Bear Lake Press* has a photo contest for the best fish picture. The prize is a fancy digital camera like the pros use. It shoots video and pictures."

I thought about the camera for a minute. If I won the photo contest, I could give the camera to Dad to replace the one I broke when Bobber and I fell off the dock.

Then I thought about Old Sam. He sure was beautiful and sleek. He was the biggest fish in White Bear Lake.

"I don't know, Chief," I said. "I kind of like the thought of Old Sam being out there. If we kill him, then there won't be a Monster of White Bear Lake anymore. Then we won't be able to fish for giants."

The Chief looked down at me and nodded, knowingly. I could tell he was thinking hard about it, too.

"A lot of people have tried to catch this fish, Spinner. Just about every one of them wants to be the one to reel in Old Sam," said The Chief, the words coming out of his mouth softly. "You, me, and Bobber, we'll always know you caught the monster."

I looked at The Chief. I could see the wisdom in his eyes.

"If we let him go, he'll be a lot harder to catch and probably die of old age. Then the Monster of White Bear Lake will be a legend forever. It's up to you, Spinner. You caught him," said The Chief.

"Aw, I don't want to be famous for killing him," I said. "Let him go, Chief."

Chapter 13

Grand Champion Anglers

Bobber and I stood on the side of the boat as we watched The Chief put Old Sam back into the water. At first, the fish just kind of moved its mouth and gills. Then its color got lighter.

The Chief held the fish by the tail, supporting its belly while keeping its head underwater.

"Last chance, Spinner," said The Chief, looking up. "You'll probably never catch a muskie this big again. You might even be able to talk your parents into making a mount of him for the wall."

"Aw, let him go, Chief," I said, as I looked over at Bobber who was fiddling with his Shoe Bait. "I don't want a fish on the wall if I have to kill it. He just looks so sad."

"As soon as I let him go, he'll look a lot different. He'll look just as mean as before," said The Chief. "Only you'll know how he really is."

I shook my head, and The Chief pushed Old Sam forward. We watched as he sank into the depths, kicking his tail ever so slowly.

"You just let the most famous fish in White Bear Lake go," said Bobber as he shook his head in disbelief. "I think I'm going to need a soda."

"I think that's a great idea," said The Chief as he turned the key and started the boat's engine. "Let's go to Tally's and get a couple of sodas, and you can tell everyone in the tackle shop about Old Sam."

We arrived at Tally's Marina, tied off the boat, and then hurried up the dock. The Chief ordered three sodas and handed one to Bobber and me. He took a long sip of his drink and then put it down on the counter.

"Hey, guys," said The Chief to the men sitting near the counter. "Who's the best fisherman on White Bear Lake?"

"There are a lot of good ones," said the man behind the counter, pointing to pictures on the wall of different anglers holding big fish. "You're one of the best I know of, Chief. There are only a couple others who have won as many tournaments as you."

"Any of them catch a muskie as big as an oar?" asked The Chief. "Or Old Sam? Have any of them caught Old Sam?"

At the mention of Old Sam, everyone in Tally's turned to face The Chief. Old Sam was serious business. Everyone wanted to be the one to catch Old Sam.

"No, Chief, none of them has caught Old Sam. Not even you," said the man behind the counter. "The person who catches Old Sam would be famous around White Bear Lake. He'd be a grand champion angler."

"Well," said The Chief with a pause. "You're looking at the grand champion anglers of White Bear Lake."

"You caught Old Sam, Chief?"

"Not me. These boys did. They worked hard to track him down, then got him on a live sucker. Held him in my hands and saw the scar on his nose myself," boasted The Chief.

"Well, where is he?" said the man. "I want to be the first to take a photo of Old Sam with these boys. You guys are going to be in the paper tomorrow, and everyone's going to know about it."

"We let him go," I said. "I didn't want to kill him. We let him go so someone else can have fun catching The Monster of White Bear Lake."

"Well, I'll be," said the man behind the counter. "Chief, these boys sure are a special breed of fisherman. They're the fishing kids from White Bear Lake."

The Chief then told the story of how we caught Old Sam and then let him go, and how dad's camera got ruined, so we couldn't take a picture. The man behind the counter just nodded and then bought us both an ice cream.

"It's a shame you guys didn't at least get a photo of Old Sam," said the nice man. "You might have won the *White Bear Lake Press* fishing photo contest with that one."

Chapter 14

FishingKids

*O*ver the next two weeks, everyone around White Bear Lake had heard about our catch. Some believed it, many didn't. Some said the only way to know was to have a photo or to bring Old Sam in to Tally's.

Bobber and I didn't care what everyone else thought. Everyone in town knew The Chief, and they knew his word was as solid as a bar of gold. Bobber and I knew we'd seen The Monster of White Bear Lake firsthand, and we had touched him with our own hands. Not many people could say they've ever done that.

Bobber and I tried several times to catch another monster muskie near his dock using suckers for bait. We caught five muskies, but all of them were less than 20 inches long. If The Monster of White Bear Lake really was Old Sam, he was probably still feeding along the shore between our houses. But we never did see him again.

I walked into the kitchen at The Chief's one day while he was sitting at the table eating lunch. On the table next to his plate was Dad's camera.

"I tried to fix it, Spinner, but no luck. We're going to need a new one," said The Chief as he pushed the camera to my side of the table. "I'll bet your dad would love one of those fancy digital cameras that shoots video and photos."

"Gosh, Chief, those are expensive. I'll have to wash every car in town to buy Dad one of those," I said, hoping The Chief would change the subject.

"They are expensive, Spinner. But your dad likes cool gadgets just like you. I'll bet he'd even let you guys borrow the camera to take photos of the fish you catch," said The Chief.

"You're right, Chief. Dad would love that camera. I'm going to earn the money to get it for him if I have to wash every car in Minnesota," I said.

The Chief just smiled and sat back in his chair. I'd seen that look before. He knew something that I didn't.

He said nothing as he picked up the paper and started reading. I sat there watching The Chief as I waited for him to share his secret.

Then I noticed a big color photo on the front page of the paper. I leaned in closer to get a better look. The caption read, "Fishing Kids Capture White Bear Lake Monster, Win Photo Contest."

The Chief looked over the top of the paper and smiled.

"It's the photo you guys took," he said. "I couldn't save the camera, but the memory card was still good. I sent it in to the photo contest."

I sat there stunned as The Chief reached under the table and pulled out a box. In it was a new camera and a plaque that read, "First Place, *White Bear Lake Press* Fishing Photo Contest."

"You're the best, Chief," I said, smiling. "I can't wait to go fishing with you again."

"Funny you should mention that, Spinner. Your Uncle Pete just retired, and he bought a new recreational vehicle and a boat to tow. He wants to take us on a trip, that is, if you don't mind fishing for something besides muskies."

I just smiled as I read the instructions for the new camera. If I was going on a fishing trip, I would need to know how to take pictures. Who knows what kind of monsters are out there waiting to be caught.

If you enjoyed Spinner and Bobber's first adventure...

Then tag along as the boys head down to the Florida Keys aboard Uncle Pete's tricked-out RV. They're on their way to fish for mahi, tarpon, wahoo, and snapper. A new friend, Coral, awaits them. Join them as they try to solve...

THE MYSTERY OF PORPOISE POINT

FiSHiNG KiDS

Available now at ...

www.FishingKids.com

Also, be sure to visit Bobber and Spinner online at...

www.FishingKids.com

- **ONLINE GAMES**
- **ACTION FIGURES**
- **FISHINGKIDS APPAREL**
- **AND FUN FOR EVERYONE!**

Mike Holliday has been a USCG licensed fishing guide out of Stuart, Florida, since 1986. He has served in editorial positions with *Florida Fishing Weekly* and *Florida Sportsman Magazine.* A renowned writer and photographer, Mike is the author of three books on inshore fishing. His writing and photography credits also include *The Miami Herald, The Palm Beach Post, The Fort Pierce Tribune, The Stuart News,* and several other local and national fishing publications.

As a fishing guide, Mike targets trophy `snook, spotted seatrout, redfish, permit, tarpon, and flounder on the Treasure Coast. Adept at leading spin, plug, and fly anglers to the catch of a lifetime, he regularly pursues his targeted species in the Indian and St. Lucie Rivers and the nearshore waters of the Atlantic Ocean.

Mike currently resides in Stuart, Florida, with his wife and three children, where they are constantly on the water and living the dream.